Sleeping On the Job

A Story of Sex and Work

Ivy Deans

COPYRIGHT

PRINT EDITION

ISBN: 978-163-5010-220

THE DOMINANT MALE, THE SUBMISSIVE FEMALE...

She was shy, she just wanted the opportunity to make her own money, to contribute to the household and take some of the pressure off of her husband. Her decision to work with a particular company throws her into the dark world of high end prostitution. The boss was a dominant man and he always got what he wanted. How do you escape from a man who wants you and wants to pimp you out to keep his business profitable...

IVY DEANS IS A WRITER who bases all her novels on things that happen in society. She continues to spend her time doing extensive research into the human condition and over the years, she has come up with quite a number of themes on which to focus. One topic that many seem to avoid is that fact that women still get themselves into highly precarious situations.

Ivy focuses on women who are focused on one goal and in the long run, they will do anything to achieve that goal. They will accept a certain deal until they get too far in to get out and then they just have to accept that reality.

HOW THE STORY UNFOLDS...

It's Just a Job

"If you're going to play a prostitute, you can't be too squeamish about that sort of thing. It's just part of the job, since the role requires it."

Paula Malcomson

DEDICATION

"This book is dedicated to all women who are stuck in a bad situation. There is always a way out. Never be blinded by subtle promises of better things to come!"

LIFE UNFOLDS

Six months ago Selena got her Master of Science Degree in Accounting and Finance with honors. She was married shortly thereafter to her partner of three years Francis. He had also been her mentor. It was a very large wedding with more than two hundred guests in attendance. She was of Indian descent so she honored her parents' wishes and they had a traditional ceremony. No expense was spared. She wore expensive outfits and priceless jewels. Thanks to her father's connections, she got the jewels to borrow from a friend of his named Raj who collected fine jewels. As such, the security was in place to ensure the jewels remained safe and that the high profile guests at the wedding were safe as well.

Raj attended the wedding with his wife Shakira. They had a bevy of personal security guards around them. These men would risk their very lives for their boss and his wife. They were treated extremely well and some were even benefiting from the opportunity to get more educated. Seated next to Raj and his wife was Stacy. She had been her classmate; she just did not have the financial or emotional support that Selena did. Stacy looked in awe at the ceremony. It was so spectacular and Selena was absolutely beautiful in all those precious jewels.

Stacy dreamed that she would have this sort of lifestyle one day. She was a newlywed as well and had married Sanjay a few months beforehand. They did not have a lot of money and she was lucky enough to get a job on campus as an administrator. It did not pay much but they got by. She was an introvert and was extremely shy. She did not have half the adventures Selena had had with her fiancé whom she later married.

Stacy could not stay home and be the housewife. That is why she had gone out and looked for a job. The economy was in a downturn, so it was extremely hard to even get an interview, much less a decent paying job. She did not have many qualifications, so it was even harder for her. A lot of her interviewers told her to go be a good stay at home wife or to go back to the land of her ancestors (India).

Though it hurt her to hear that she was not suitable for the job, she kept on trying. She went to interview after interview and none of them went in her favor. She had one favor she could ask, but she did not want to use it. She could ask Selena to help her get something; to talk to one of her colleagues to give her a job.

She was in another interview. She was again being told that there were no entry level jobs available. She just wanted to get up and leave, but she sat there listening to the excuses being given. Wait what was that? Did he just say a position was being created?

She started to listen more keenly. She was being asked if she would be interested in that position when it became available.

"What does the job entail?"

"Simple customer service, you would have to deal with customers that have problems. The aim is to solve it quickly, to retain the customer and to have them refer us because we solve problems quickly."

"I would be extremely interested in that job sir."

"Fantastic. The job has a probationary period. During that time we will evaluate you to make sure that you are a perfect fit for the job. I will train you and you will report directly to me. You need to be here by 8:30 am tomorrow. Right now I will give you a quick tour of the offices and hand you over to human resources to fill out the necessary paperwork. Lateness is not accepted."

"I can do that. How do I address you sir?"

"Sir will suffice for now."

"Okay sir, no problem."

This was fantastic; she could not wait to give her husband the news. It would not be much, but she would be able to contribute something to the household. She got to work extremely early the next morning, not wanting to be late. She went right to her boss's office and knocked. She had taken time to get ready, putting on a black pants suit and a bit of makeup. She thought it was quite appropriate for the job.

"Come in."

Her boss Mr. Flynn was looking at her with disdain. She wondered what she had done wrong already.

"What is that you are wearing? Are you in mourning? We want happy customers, not depressed ones."

"I am sorry," she stammered, "I thought it would be appropriate. Can you tell me what to wear from now on?"

"We are going to fix the problem right now. I am taking you shopping and I will get you the outfits you should be wearing. They will serve as your uniforms, so don't worry, it will be at the company's expense.

Stacy was quiet. She had nothing to say. The company would be paying for the clothes, so she would wear whatever he bought. She followed him out and he carried her to a clothing store. It was pretty high end. She had passed it many times but did not go in as she could not afford anything in there. He picked a number of outfits for her to try on. She had to put on each one and show him how she looked in them. He preferred outfits that accentuated her figure, something that would hold the attention of the customers.

"Sir, it can't be too sexy, I am married and have to respect my husband."

"My dear Stacy, being married does not mean that you are dead. That is what happened in the golden ages."

"I am not dead sir."

Finally, he saw what he liked. He opted for a close fitting pencil skirt and a blouse that showed a lot of cleavage. The two pieces alone were extremely expensive. She started to protest at the price, but he would have none of it. He paid for it and told her to go put it on right away. She did and got a bag to put the outfit she had worn to work in. She was ready to face the work day and followed Mr. Flynn out of the store. She soon realized that they were not headed back to the office.

He headed to another high end clothing store. This was for the real high end clientele. There were comfortable chairs and it was decorate with expensive carpets and furniture. Out of nowhere, a store clerk appeared and asked how he may help.

Mr. Flynn asked for shoes to go with the new outfit he had just bought.

The clerk looked at her making her slightly uncomfortable. After staring at her intensely for a few minutes, he turned to Mr. Flynn and said, "She has beautiful long legs, a pair of high heels would be great. For the rainy weather that we are so prone to, a nice pair of knee high boots would go well with that outfit."

"Sounds like what I had in mind. Tell the clerk your shoe size and try on the shoe so I can see how you look in them."

He selected the six inch heels. She could barely walk in them. He took the bags from her that had in her modest outfit and sensible shoes. As they walked by a dustbin, he threw them in."

"My clothes and shoes Mr. Flynn! Why did you throw them away?"

"That is where they deserve to be Stacy. Don't you ever let me see you in such a drab, unflattering outfit ever again?"

She nodded. She had spent all her money on the outfit. She would just appreciate the replacement as it was gorgeous. The next problem that Mr. Flynn had was that he could see her bra through the blouse. Slowly but surely, he was controlling her and it was only the first day of work. The next store they went in was a lingerie store. She had to try on numerous bras, but he still complained that they were visible.

"I have an idea. Go back in the changing room and remove your bra. You are young and I think your breasts will look quite fine without a bra."

She went to do as he requested. What had she signed up for? She would comply for now as they really needed the money.

She went out to let him see her and he was satisfied with her. She felt naked and thought she looked like a high priced call girl.

"Not a thing is wrong with you my dear. Your breasts are nice and perky and those unsightly bra lines are gone.

It was now lunchtime. She could not believe that they had been away from the office all morning.

"Well Stacy, might as well grab a bite to eat before getting back to the office eh! There is a great restaurant around the block."

"Okay sir."

She felt good and she noticed that she was being looked at by the young and old men she passed. She was walking better in the shoes and she held her head high and strut her stuff. She even got a few whistles from the younger ones. Finally they got to the restaurant; the waiter greeted them and led them to a secluded table for two. Mr. Flynn ordered some drinks for them and she thought she saw him exchanging knowing looks with the waiter. Maybe it was just her imagination. She put her unease at rest and decided to enjoy the lunch.

The drinks came to the table and she had a sip of it. It was quite a nice blend of exotic fruits. It was supposed to be fruit juice but somehow she felt tipsy. Her boss was drinking his, and seemed to have no problems so she kept drinking.

Soon she finished that drink and Mr. Flynn beckoned to the waiter to bring another. He was talking to her and saying how beautiful she was, but he sounded so far away. She did not even know that the drink had liquor in it. The second one had even more in it. She was talking but her words were garbled. She was so out of it that she did not react in any way when Mr. Flynn started to kiss her. He also put his hand on her thigh and she did nothing.

Soon she said she had to go to the ladies room. He got up to show her where to go. He followed her, guiding her to the bathroom. She went in used the facilities and came out to see him waiting for her. He helped her back to the table. She was succumbing to the effects of the liquor. She was drunk. He was now kissing her again and he had placed both hands on her breast and he was squeezing them. He kissed her again and she did not object. His tongue was in her mouth. She let him kiss her, seemingly unaware of what was happening to her.

He had achieved his objective; she was like putty in his hands. He leaned in and told her he was going to take her panties off. She had no objections. The underwear was off and he got her to pull her skirt up so she was naked from the waist down. Her boss had full view of her pussy and her legs were apart so he got a good view. He took a series of pictures of her with her skirt up; he also took pictures of her face and of her with her blouse open. He got all the pictures that he needed. He had more than enough ammunition to control this bitch. He made her button up and pull down her skirt before the waiter came back to check on the table.

She soon found out that they had other stops to make before they went back to the office. She was still drunk as a skunk, but she had no objection to anything her boss was ordering her to do. By the end of the day she had a new hairdo and she had had every hair waxed off her body. Her boss had told her that if her husband had any issues with the changes, she should just let him know that it was all for him. She was working now and she could be the woman that she wanted to be for him.

She was sufficiently sober by the time her husband got home from work. She felt different and knew a lot had happened throughout the day but some of it was a blur. Her head ached a bit but she put on a brave smile for her husband. Sanjay was turned on by her new look and her newly waxed pussy was very appealing to him.

After a few days at the office Stacy soon discovered that her boss loved the outdoors. He had an athletic build and participated in lots of sporting activities. He started to teach her many things. She learned to surf and she had to improve her swimming skills beforehand. He was still taking her shopping. She even got what she can only refer to as a bare as you dare swimsuit, as it left nothing to the imagination. Strangely enough she did not find the extra attention strange. She simply thought that her boss was trying to make her as comfortable as possible. Little did she know that he had much more sinister plans in mind for her?

He told her she had to be sexy for the customers. He wanted her to be bolder with her outfits. She was no longer allowed to wear a bra, as it was too noticeable. He also did not want her to wear panties anymore. He hated seeing the lines as they were distracting. It was just weird that she followed whatever her boss said without objection. Maybe it was how he said it. In fact he had taken off the panties himself. As far as he was concerned, she was to be appealing to the customer. She sometimes wondered who these customers were and why she had to be so sexy for them.

It did not bother her as much as it should. He planned more shopping trips, as he wanted to dress her in more revealing blouses and shorter skirts. The skirts were so short that one wrong move would reveal her pussy to whoever was looking.

She continued to agree to whatever he said despite being warned by other women in the office that he used women and treated them like he owned them. She also knew that numerous women in the office had given birth to his children. He certainly looked the part. He was handsome and he was a man who cared about his appearance. He did not have an ounce of fat anywhere at all.

REELING HER IN

Mr. Flynn had her doing a lot of things. One thing that he had her do, was to practice to walk in a certain way. Of course it was for the customers. He would sit and watch her and instruct her on how to seem seductive as she walked and how to make her but jiggle without it seeming gross. As soon as she got that down, he also taught her how to make her breast move a certain way when she walked. The lack of a bra made it that much easier. He made her do it again and again until he was satisfied that she had mastered it.

When he was done, she had a look at herself walk in a full length mirror. She hardly recognized herself. The girl who had once been clunking about was suddenly a sensuous siren. Even her husband had noticed the changes and how much more seductive she seemed. He was much more interested in spending more time with her and to go out with her. He was making the extra effort.

Her boss also continued to give her surfing lessons in the automated wave pool that was in the office. She was sure that he just wanted to have closer contact with her, why he volunteered to do that. This was the same boss who had changed the way she dressed and had disputed the need for any undergarments at all.

He had insisted that she wear the barely there swimsuit for the lessons. It did attract all the men in the office who suddenly seemed obligated to pass by the wave pool when she was there. Her nipples were extremely sensitive and poked out as more cold water hit her. She knew everyone could see and she was embarrassed. Her boss had seen that, and insisted that it was because she was attracted to him why her nipples were hard.

She saw that he was joking so she laughed it off as he looked at her inquisitively. She was a diligent student. She fell off the board quite a number of times. She was tired and just wanted out. She tried to get her boss to let her rest and try another day when she was in better shape.

She was of course chided for being lazy.

"I am not lazy sir, I do get exercise, my husband and I go jogging every morning."

"Oh you need more than that. You should increase the time you jog and incorporate some other routines in your workout regime. You will get stronger if you do that."

"Wouldn't I need a personal trainer sir; can you help me with that?"

"I would be delighted. Well let's get started shall we."

He led her to the gym and started her on some cardio. He then had her focus on working out her arms and her abs and legs. He chided her for being so young and not having a flat stomach. He was not being kind with his statements. Surprisingly she was not offended by his statements. She had gotten used to his crude way of saying things. He was a man who said what he meant, no matter who it hurt.

After putting her through a rigorous workout, he told her she could relax in the sauna for a bit. As she headed toward the door he stopped her, advising her to take the suit off as it would shrink in the heat.

"But I have nothing else to put on Mr. Flynn!"

"Don't worry about it. I won't look." He turned around to give her the opportunity to take the suit off.

I will take off what I have on too if that will make you more comfortable. She blushed and took the suit off. She literally ran into the sauna. He had taken off his clothes and joined her in the sauna. He was a brazen one. She was not bothered at all by this.

"You are a cheeky one Mr. Flynn!"

"That may be so Stacy but like fine wine I get better at it as I get older. Do you know how beautiful you look naked?"

She blushed. He never seemed to have a problem talking like that to a woman. He was talking as if they were casually chatting about a pair of shoes or lunch options. He was skilled at flirting. It was different though, as it did not seem brash like some of the men she had met while in college. He was very debonair with his charm. She must admit that she liked it.

He moved closer to her and he put his arm around her. She did not flinch. She was happy so he could do anything he wanted at this point. He was whispering sweet nothings in her ear. He was saying all the right things and she was enjoying his charm. Every woman wanted to be told that she was beautiful! He was becoming bolder now. He was playing with her ear, teasing it with his tongue. She was turned on. She did not protest. Her body language indicated that he could do that and more if he wanted. She just made the decision to enjoy the moment.

Her eyes were closed and she pictured herself. She loved Sean Connery so she imagined that they were on a deserted tropical island and that he was making his move. She imagined him caressing her body, playing with her breasts, kissing her all over. He was kissing her roughly on the mouth. Suddenly she felt his hand at her crotch. He was playing with the lips of her vagina. She knew that it was Mr. Flynn doing it and that she should object but she was yearning for it. Her body was yielding to his touches.

He kept on doing what he was doing. He was kissing her, his tongue probing her mouth. This was perfect. It was a moment that she had been dreaming of for a long time. She felt his fingers entering her pussy. It was dripping wet. He was working his fingers like an expert, making her even wetter. He withdrew his fingers and sucked them. He put his other hand and she started to suck his fingers. She opened her eyes and looked right at him. She was daring him with her eyes to do something else.

He took his hand out of his mouth and went back to teasing her pussy. He found her clit and teased it. He started to suck her nipples. She arched her back in response to his advances. It was delightful. She was fully aroused and wanted more. She did not care that it was not her husband that was pleasing her. This man had total control of her. He was proving that minute by minute. She had been unfaithful to her husband Sanjay but that was out the door now. Her inhibitions were gone. She wanted this man badly.

He intensified his motions, ripening her clit harder causing her breath to catch in her throat. She was in heaven. She was close to having an orgasm. He was so good with his fingers; she could only imagine what else he could do. She was getting louder and louder. She covered her mouth with her hands as other people were in the vicinity. She did that not a moment too soon as she had the most powerful orgasm that she had ever had. She was shaking like a leaf. It was perfect. As she recovered, Mr. Flynn was kissing her and caressing her face.

"How was that Stacy? Did you enjoy it?"

She could not speak, she nodded. She wanted more. She could see that he was aroused as well. He ended it at that point and told her to go and shower and get dressed.

Years went by and they kept having these impromptu make out sessions, he was always in charge, leaving her wanting more at the end. She sought that satisfaction from her husband when she got home. Soon enough, she was pregnant with twins. She had them and successfully settled into being a mother. She started to exercise again and was soon back in perfect shape. She was back at work after three months, leaving her babies in the care of a highly recommended nanny who was being supervised by her mother.

INITIATION

Mr. Flynn was happy she was back and that she had not forgotten what she was taught. Her breasts were fuller after childbirth, making them even more appealing. She also had a fuller shape as she had matured over the years. He soon took up where he left off.

Soon he invited her to his house. His girlfriend was on a business trip so he was free to carry in whom he pleased. They barely got in the door when he made her take off her clothes. He took off his as well and his dick was fully erect. He was ogling her like a schoolboy seeing a naked woman for the first time. She was ripe and ready for the taking. He led her to the couch and started to play with her breasts. She had her legs open and he pushed his fingers into her vagina. It was wet, she was ready for him. Her breathing was labored; she wanted him to ravage her.

He pushed her down onto the cushions and positioned himself over her. His cock was huge. Much bigger than her husbands, she wondered if he would be able to penetrate her. He played with her clit making her gush fluid. She was on cloud nine. She never knew that she could feel like this. He moved his dick closer to her pussy, gently entering her, allowing her fluids to lubricate his cock. He took his time. This was perfect. She had yielded to his plan perfectly so far, without knowing what. His true intentions were. He pushed his cock in slowly allowing her to get used to him. He made it all the way in and he stayed there for a bit allowing her pussy to adjust. She was tight indeed. He started to move in and out slowly. He continued to play with her breasts. She willed him to grab them, to squeeze them harder. He had no objections.

He quickened the pace. She was moaning uncontrollably. He suddenly stopped and led her to the bedroom. He pushed her down on the bed and climbed on to her. He leaned forward and flipped a switch. It turned on his hidden camera that would show her face as she enjoyed another man pleasuring her. He entered her again and started to fuck her. He was going faster and faster until he was ramming her. She was losing her mind, it felt so good. She was sure the neighbors could hear her. He kept on ramming her. The bed was literally bouncing on the carpet. He was enjoying this. He would cum soon. He could feel his dick swelling. He started to moan, ramming her faster and faster, touching her cervix every time. He suddenly pushed himself deep inside her and stopped. He roared as he came, filling her pussy with his seed.

He rolled off her when he was done, sperm still oozing from his dick. She smiled and said she would go have a bath and get back to work. He shook his head and made her go take the bath, put on the outfit she saw in the bathroom and come back to bed. She did as he ordered. In the bathroom he had left sexy red and black lace lingerie that left nothing to the imagination.

She had a bath, put it on and rejoined him in the bedroom. He was almost asleep. She lay down beside him and soon they were both sleeping. They woke up in the afternoon, refreshed after a long nap. Stacy could feel his dick poking her in her side. He was fully awake in every sense of the word.

"Stacy, my dick is hard, fuck me now!"

She said nothing. She slipped out of the bottom half of the lingerie. She started to give him a hand job, moving her hand up and down his dick, feeling it swell in her hands. He was moaning softly. He started to fondle her breasts through the lingerie. His other hand soon found her clit and he started to tease it, stopping to push his finger in. She was turned on. He could feel her juices running. She continued to give him the hand job.

When she could take it no longer she climbed on top of him, straddling him. Slowly she started to lower herself onto him. His dick was really big. How had she managed the first time? She took her time, giving her pussy the time to adjust. He was eager to be inside her. He started to push his dick in slowly. He took his time so he would not cause her to tear. Soon he was all in. He gave her a moment to adjust to his size, pulling her down to kiss her fervently on the mouth. She was moaning softly, her eyes were closed. He started to thrust, picking up the pace gradually. He was going to fuck her to death.

She was enjoying every minute of it. She started to move up and down in time with his thrusts. They were going faster and faster, the bed was making noise again, the faster they went, the louder the bed got and the louder their moans got. Pretty soon she felt the sensation building up inside her. She was on the verge of another big orgasm. She stopped moving and held onto him a he continued to thrust. Soon her body was rocked by a gigantic orgasm. He could feel her pussy contracting. He was going to cum. He kept thrusting and he came violently. He was spent. She got off him, his seed spilling out of her.

"Come on Stacy, suck my dick, and let me see how good you are!"

She grabbed his dick and started to suck. She cleaned the cum off and kept on working.

"Yes, that is the way to do it!"

"Your husband should be happy with you. You have a special skill. As soon as you deal with your first customer, you will be on staff permanently. I will go with you to make sure there are no hitches. After that you are on your own."

"Thank you sir, I have been waiting for this opportunity for a long time."

"No problem. You will do that and you will continue to satisfy my demands."

"What sir! I can't sleep with you again. I have a husband. I only did what I did to ensure I would get to keep the job. The aim was not to upset you."

"Your plan worked. I was not going to keep you, but you have proven yourself. You get a lot of perks with this job you know. The pay is above average, you get clothing and shoe allowance plus you get to go to the salon to become even more beautiful. You will also continue to dine at the best restaurants in the country. Would you want it to be any different?"

He drove a hard bargain. He planned to mold her into what he really wanted. Well it was the opportunity to live like Selena and Shakira. She had always been jealous that they had all they wanted, first from their parents and now from their husbands.

Pretty soon, Stacy was Mr. Flynn's girlfriend on the side. He was in total control of her. He told her what she was to wear and when she was to wear it. Even when he was not with her, she had his orders on how to dress. She was a bit rounded by this at first but after a while it was just another quirk that her boss had. She loves her husband dearly but her boss was the one in charge as he was the one paying her.

The annual company party was coming up and Stacy was expected to be there with her husband. It started off okay. She went in with Sanjay and they were both greeted warmly by her boss. He kissed her hand gallantly. She was terrified at how it might look, but Sanjay thought it was nice. She decided to enjoy the party and spent the time dancing with Sanjay.

Soon enough, her boss cut in, "sir, I humbly request a dance with your charming wife."

Sanjay laughed and handed her over to her boss. She looked at him with pleading eyes, but his attention had already been captured by a platinum blonde haired beauty who was dancing with him as if her life depended on it. Why was she so upset by this? After all, she was sleeping with her boss to keep her job and enjoy all the luxuries to which she had become accustomed. He should have gone to sit down and wait for her to finish dancing with her boss. He would get it from her when the evening was through!

She would show her husband why he should not look at any other women. She pushed herself onto her boss. Her low cut dress shifted and he could stare right down at her huge breasts. The dress clung to her like it was molded to her body. That is what her boss liked her to wear and that was the outfit he had told her to wear to the party. She knew she was looking like a sexy siren so why shouldn't she act like it. She moved even closer to her boss, rubbing herself against him in full view. If the lights were any brighter it would had revealed her every bold move. Her boss held onto her. She could feel his cock growing larger and larger, fighting to get out of his pants. There she was dancing with her boyfriend who just happened to be her boss, a few feet away from her husband. She continued to dance. Her boss was rubbing his dick against her. She was getting hot, she was turned on.

Her nipples were huge. With every rub they got as her boss twirled her around, she became more aroused. He used the opportunity of the darkened room to lower one hand to her crotch. He started to rub her through the dress. Her senses were heightened. She could barely control her moans. She was pushing against his hand, willing him to make her cum; pretty soon she did, burying her face in his neck. Her legs felt like jelly. If he had not been holding onto her tightly, she would have dropped to the ground like a sack of flour.

He led her off the dance floor and down the corridor to his office. He turned and locked the door behind him. She felt like a high school girl at prom. This was the moment you snuck off with your boyfriend to make out. She literally pounced on him. She wanted him and she wanted him now. He was grabbing her roughly. Kissing her like she had never been kissed before and he was teasing her very wet pussy.

He cleared the papers off of his table and motioned for her to get on the desk. She did not have on any panties. She had told Sanjay that she did not want persons looking at the lines; it would be a distraction that he would not like. She opened up her legs, showing her boss that she was ready for him. He merely zipped done and pulled out his engorged dick. It was fully erect, needing a warm, wet pussy to envelope it.

He started to enter her, moving slowly. She was eager to have him so she lifted up her dress and pushed herself forward until he was all in. She started to move, his head was buried in her ample bosom. He made her lean back so he could fuck her. He thrust hard, moving his dick in and out of her wet dripping pussy. He touched her cervix with every thrust. She was screaming for him to fuck her harder.

"Sir, you know what to do, fuck me...harder, harder, I want all of you inside me sir!"

This was enough to spur him on. He rammed her harder and harder until he came inside her. She came shortly thereafter, screaming loudly. He waited for her spasms to subside. He pulled out and watched his cum leak out of her. That was always a turn on.

"Clean up; let me talk to you for a minute." He had already wiped off his dick and had zipped up.

She grabbed some tissues, wiped up the cum and hopped off the desk, pulling her dress down.

"You are ready to really get into the customer service job now Stacy."

"Finally, I thought that I was only here for your personal satisfaction. I can get some real work done."

"You have to go out into the world eventually. I just had to be sure that you were ready to do this. I have an especially difficult client that I want you to convince to keep doing business with us."

"Happy to be of service Mr. Flynn!"

"Okay, he is from Spain and he will be here next week. He is complaining about the last large shipment that we sent to him. The equipment has not met his full requirements. It is not much of a difference, but I do not want him to lean toward returning the shipment."

"Okay, shall I offer him a discount or some other product as a bonus to sweeten the deal?"

"I have already agreed to reduce the price. He has made complaints before, but we have always been able to work it out. I can tell you what he likes, women. He loves to have those high priced call girls visiting his hotel room. It is a rather costly exercise. I think that you can help me out with that."

"What, you want me to fuck him! Is that why I am here? So you can pimp me out to customers so they take your inferior products. I won't do it!"

"I would think carefully before I talk my dear. I can always advise your husband of what you have been doing."

She was now scared. This was what blackmail felt like. He had the upper hand. She could never let Sanjay find out what she had been doing. He would kick her out and divorce her. Where would she be then?"

"As I was saying, I will go with you and stay with you through the first encounter. After that, you should be able to handle things yourself. He knows how to please women; he has made it an art so you will enjoy the experience."

She nodded and followed him back to the party. She sulked for the rest of the evening. Sanjay was jumping through hoops to try to please her thinking he had made her upset. She shrugged him off. Eventually pulling herself together to dance with him and not make him suspicious.

She was ready to go home. They had to say goodbye to her boss. Sanjay shook his hand thanking him for a delightful evening. Mr. Flynn hugged her; he pressed something into her palm.

He whispered into her ear, "go and get some new clothes and some good lingerie. He must be impressed and I want the receipts for whatever you bought."

She was in shock. Why was he treating her like this? She was nothing to him but a paid private whore. He made her and he could break her. Strangely she was turned on by the idea. She had given in to Sanjay's wish to have a threesome not too long ago. She was more open to different things sexually. Her husband was pleased, so was her lover and that turned her on. Now she would be charming the big clients, putting on her charm and opening her pussy to keep business booming for her boss.

She started to prepare for the meeting. She took her lunch time to go and check out all the shops. She looked for the most alluring dress, slutty but not off-putting. She found an outfit that suited her perfectly. Her bosom would look perfect in it. Next she got some killer shoes to go with the dress. She then went to find the lingerie. That could be as slutty as she wanted as it would not be revealed until her dress was off. She opted for a black and white number. It was not much material but it put the focus on the essential areas.

THE FIRST THREESOME

It was the day of the meeting and she dressed carefully, making sure that she would get the approval of her boss. They were meeting at a restaurant first. She got there at the appointed time and asked for the Flynn party. She was helped out of her coat by the waiter and a hush fell on the area. All eyes were on her. She was stunning in her sizzling red dress with cut outs in all the right places. She was much more conservatively dressed in her own home.

She walked in the sultry way that she was taught to drawing the eyes of men and women as she was escorted to the table. She could see Mr. Flynn sitting with two other gentlemen. He stood up as she approached. The other gentlemen turned around and stood up as well. He greeted her and then introduced her to the gentlemen. The older of the two was Mr. Gutierrez, the man with the complaint; the other was one of his managers, Mr. Smith. She had seen black men before, but Mr. Smith was well built and had chocolate smooth skin.

After getting through the introduction, they got down to the business aspect of the evening. The two gentlemen looked at her from time to time, taking it all in. They were looking at her boss with greedy eyes and they smiled at her appreciatively. She was sitting in between the two of them so they got more than an eyeful each time they looked at her.

She wondered if Mr. Smith's dick was bigger than her bosses. She had heard stories and wondered if they were true. The waiter came to the table and they ordered their meal. It was a fantastic selection and Mr. Flynn insisted that only the best wine be served with the meal. After dessert, Mr. Gutierrez was in the mood for dancing so they went to a club that catered to older gentlemen like him. She realized that she was really just there to do his bidding, no matter what it was. He led her out to the dance floor using it as an opportunity to look at her even more closely and to grope her.

After satisfying himself, he turned her over to Mr. Smith. He was just as bad with the groping and flirting. She was tipsy and they kept on getting her drinks. They went back to their private booth and sat down and the drinks kept coming. Mr. Gutierrez started to kiss her, forcing his tongue into her mouth.

He sat down and started to run his hands up her dress. He was grabbing her butt and pushing his hands into her panties. He made her lift her dress and sit down; he was rubbing her pussy not caring who saw. She was reacting to what he was doing. He knew what he was doing. She was dripping wet. Gutierrez gave Flynn a look and he gave a knowing nod. After ordering her to fix her clothes, he signaled for the waiter and asked for the bill. He paid the tab and they left to head to the hotel where he had reserved a suite.

Mr. Flynn went ahead to check in while the gentlemen got to know Stacy better.

As they headed up in the elevator they were looking at her greedily. Mr. Gutierrez pulled off her panties so he could get a better grip on her pussy. The elevator stopped and they walked quickly to the room. As soon as they got inside, they told her to get out of the dress. Before she even realized it, she was just standing there in her six inch killer heels. Gutierrez took charge. He led her to the bed. He was already out of his pants and underwear and had shrugged off his jacket. He rammed his dick into her and started to fuck her hard. Her breath caught in her throat. Now she knew why he had done the foreplay beforehand, he just wanted to get right to work. She was moaning loudly. He continued to ram her hard. She had a mind blowing orgasm. He might be old but he sure knew what he was doing.

He kept on fucking her hard. She was wet and juicy to him. Soon he stopped and beckoned to Smith. He took over. He was not ramming her as hard but he was still a good fuck. That was how it went for the next half hour or so. Gutierrez fucked her for a few minutes then Smith fucked her for a few minutes. They were relentless. They fucked her on her back and then they made her kneel down. They took a break and then went back to her. They were calling her a whole host of names. She was a bitch, a slut, a whore, a fucking Indian cunt. She should have been offended but it was a turn on for her. This whole experience since she started working for her boss had made her learn a whole lot about herself. It was crazy.

She just kneeled there letting them have their way with her. While one fucked her, the other laid down in front of her for her to suck his dick. That is how it went, they kept taking turns. Things changed when Gutierrez grabbed the lubricant. He lubed up her ass pretty good and rubbed some on his dick as well. Suddenly he started to push his engorged dick into her ass. She had never felt pain like this before. She had to grit her teeth and bear the pain. They were taking all of her. Soon after fucking her in the ass for a few minutes he came. Smith also came in her mouth.

She thought that was it but they were not done. They simply rested for a bit and then resumed. They both seemed to like fucking her in the ass. They jumped from her ass to her pussy and back again. She could say nothing; when they were taking yet another break after cumming about three more times in succession she asked if the problem had been solved.

"Not just yet you cunt," Gutierrez said, "let me fuck you again and then I will sign what I need to sign."

She simply opened up her legs and invited them to fuck her some more. They both took turns again. They had just finished ass fucking her and hadn't even wiped off before they jumped back in her pussy. After they came again and were duly satisfied. They wiped off, got dressed, Gutierrez signed the document and they left. She was badly in need of a shower.

Flynn came in from the other side of the suite. She headed into the shower to wash the men off and he joined her. His dick was rock hard. Her husband would never be able to satisfy her like he could. He fucked her right there in the shower. She had two orgasms and could barely stand. They finished their shower and got dressed and left. He dropped her home.

She went in, her husband was still out, she went to have another shower to really wash off the three men who had fucked her raw. She got dressed and sat waiting for her husband to return.

Double Duty

When she got to work the next morning Mr. Flynn was waiting on her. He had a big smile on his face.

"My client is extremely pleased. How do you feel, was it fun for you?"

She had to take a minute to formulate an answer.

"To be quite honest, I did not like how things were going at first. When they settled down to what they were doing, it was much better for me. Not sure if you were looking but they fucked me in turns, then they fucked me at the same time; one in my ass and the other in my pussy. They talked dirty, calling me nasty names. Strangely enough, I liked it and was even more aroused by it. I was even wetter than before. They fucked me for two hours straight. They took a break to rest up and to have some drinks. I was not offered any and then they started to fuck me again, turning me in all kinds of positions, some I had never heard of before."

"Well, your pussy really appealed to them."

Stacy laughed, "Well I know Gutierrez loved my pussy but Smith really got off fucking me in the ass."

"It was good for them. We achieved our goal. They have cancelled the complaints and have made and even larger order than the first one. You have more than exceeded my expectations. You can expect a nice bonus next pay day and I am going to have HR get a company credit card for you."

"Thank you sir, it is more than I could ever have expected. Something seems to be bothering you though. Is there anything that I can do to help?"

"Well, just having you in the office has made me quite horny. My dick is as hard as a rock. What can you do to help with that?"

"Sir, I can give you a blow job, if that is okay with you."

He pushed the chair back. From his desk to give her room and told her to lock the office door. She was so nervous. She had done this so many times before and she was acting as if it was all new to her. She got undressed as he liked to see her naked and started sucking his dick. She was quite the expert by now, so he was enjoying what she was doing. He shifted so the he could play with her pussy. He rubbed the clit and then stuck some fingers in her pussy. She had become accustomed to his large dick and she was able to take much more in without gagging. That felt good. He continued to finger fuck her. She was moaning and pushing back on his fingers as he was touching her in the right places. She pushed back harder until she had an orgasm.

Now she wanted his dick to be inside of her.

"Oh sir, fuck me, I need your long hard cock inside of me!"

He spun her around, lodging her at the hips and pushed himself into her.

"Ah yes, that is what I want, fuck me hard sir!"

He was ramming her hard. She could hardly contain herself; she was feeling so much pleasure. He kept on fucking her hard and when he felt that he was about to have an orgasm. He pulled out and said in a guttural voice, "Stacy suck my cock now!"

No sooner than she had started to suck him, he came in her mouth. She created a vacuum with her mouth and not a drop of cum was wasted. She loved tasting his cum. He turned her back around, he was still hard and he started to fuck her again. So she was screaming loudly, not caring who in the office could hear. She started to shake and she starts to push back hard as he thrust forward. She kept on crying for him to go harder and faster, harder and faster, pretty soon she clamped her hand over her own mouth to hold in her screams as she came. He was playing with her breasts. He was fully erect again and knew that he had another orgasm left in him. He held onto her to prevent her from moving. He kept on thrusting, going faster and faster until he cried out.

"Fuck, I am going to cum soon, can you feel it?"

He came inside her, his cum spilling out of her pussy. She was right on track with him and had her third orgasm for the evening.

After cleaning up, she went out to sort out her desk quickly. Everyone else had left already, so her screams during lovemaking had fallen on an empty building. Mr. Flynn soon came out of his office and offered to give her a drive home. She was still extremely horny. How could this make her feel so sexy, so free? She reached over and touched his dick. It was hard so she knew he wanted her again. She zipped his pants down and started to play with it as he drove. He had to focus really hard to prevent an accident. She lifted up her dress and started to play with her pussy as well. It was throbbing hard, needing a cock to be inside it.

As soon as he pulled up at her home he pulled her into the house quickly. He hadn't even bothered to zip his pants back up. Thankfully, her husband would be out for another three hours. She closed the door behind them hastily.

"I am horny as hell sir; I need someone to fuck me now, to fuck me hard!"

Her boss had no objections to this at all. He was hard and ready to do some damage. He threw her down on the sofa and climbed over her. He positioned himself and entered her quickly. He was not taking any prisoners. He was going all out, giving her a hardcore fuck, not caring if he hurt her or not. She bucked and writhed under him, gritting her teeth as he rammed her. It hurt but it felt so damn good at the same time. She felt that she was going to have a huge orgasm; this was the biggest one yet. She screamed passionately. This encouraged Mr. Flynn to go harder and faster, they came in unison. It was such a big orgasm for her that she had passed out. Not waiting for her to recover, Mr. Flynn cleaned up all the cum off the sofa, wiped down her pussy and set her properly in the couch. He did a quick check to make sure everything was in order and he left.

She woke up just minutes before Sanjay got home. She was able to have a quick shower just in case there were any traces of her boss left in her. He had done a pretty good job of cleaning up.

"Hey honey, how was your day? Did you have any success with your troubled customers?"

"It was fantastic; I was able to convince them that they would be making a mistake if they cancelled their order with us. I'll just say that my boss was over the moon that I was able to pull it off. I should get a nice bonus at the end of the month."

"There you go, you always apply yourself to whatever task you are given. Now I am home, I feel turned on and I want you right now."

"You can have me Sanjay but I have had a long day, do you want to fuck me or do you just want one of my mind blowing blow jobs?"

"Oh honey I want to fuck you, I want you to ride me to kingdom come."

"Oh you want me to do all the work eh. I need to challenge you more often at this rate."

Sanjay smiled, "you can challenge me anytime you want."

She helped him to get undressed and he lay down on the bed. She took off her nightgown and climbed on top of him...

SUBMISSION

After an action packed week, it was a relief when Stacy found out that the next week would be fairly quiet. She still had to have sex with her boss twice daily; when she got to work and at close of day. It was pretty routine now. She wore her underwear from home to allay any suspicions that Sanjay may have. She took them off in the car when she got to the office and then she went in. She just got wet thinking that her boss was inside waiting for her, waiting to push his hand into her pussy and playing with it until it was wet enough to receive his dick.

She also kept up her beauty regimen, getting regular waxes at the spa as he did not want to see any hair at all on her cunt. She endured the pain for him. Soon another job was on the horizon, she would be meeting with another gentleman, locally based, who had issues with the time in which the orders were delivered. She was to get him to withdraw their complaint and get that negative review off of the company.

She prepared as she did for the first encounter. She went shopping for the right outfit and set of undergarments and shoes. She would not be having dinner with this gentleman. It would be straight to the hotel to get down to business. Mr. Flynn had his chauffeur drop her at the hotel where she was to me the client. She only had a room number and nothing else. She had to think for a moment that she was nothing but a high priced whore for this man.

She was surely dressed like one. It was all covered by a rather expensive coat.

One lesson that she had learned from her boss in the last few weeks was that she should never let anyone but the client see her dressed like a slut. She always put on the ultra sexy outfits and then covered them with a nice coat, something very conservative. She was wearing a sexy lingerie set, a dark blue bustier with matching crotch less panties. This was what her boss thought would appeal to that particular client.

The Sadistic Beast

She took the elevator to the appointed floor and walked down the hall until she found the room number. She knocked and soon after the door opened and she saw a burly looking Caucasian man. He was rather big, like he had been a laborer all his life. He was not into much talking she imagined, as he was told he would get a girl and there she was, ready for whatever he had in store. He seemed to be the sort of man that just fucked and left. He did not seem to have a caring bone in his body.

He beckoned for her to come barely moving out of the way so she had to push past him.

"Get naked bitch!"

Huh, Stacy had never experienced this before. She was apparently moving too slowly and he grabbed her hand roughly and slapped her.

"I said get naked now whore or I can tear all your fucking clothes off and you go home naked when I am done with you."

She thought that this was crude. She hurried however to get out of the clothes before he could get the opportunity to rip them off. She kept on the crotch less panties and matching suspenders. He wanted those to stay on as she was a slut so she should dress the part. Soon he started to grope her, he grabbed her breast roughly, he was almost pulling her nipples off, he was so rough, and tears were running down Stacy's face. He grabbed her pulling her to him and he kissed her roughly. She could only think that he had never really had a sensuous sexual experience or he just loved to be sadistic. She was sure it was the latter.

He pushed her legs apart and rammed his fingers into her pussy. She flinched.

Strangely enough, she was wet after all of that rough treatment. She had really become the slut on call, as a normal woman would never react in that way unless she was a bit sadistic herself and liked it rough. He had three of his big fingers rammed into her pussy. She was really getting a big pussy from all the big dicks that were fucking her. At one point in her life three fingers would be a lot to deal with, now she could barely feel them. She stole a glance into the mirror. Her pussy was a gaping hole, waiting for another big dick to invade it. Her poor dear husband would be lost in it if he fucked her now.

Instinctively she knelt down in front of him. She pulled his belt, zipped his pants down to see what she would have to deal with. He had a monstrous dick and it was fully erect. She just had to suck it for a few minutes to make it really hard. She was just about to shift so he could start to fuck her when he grabbed her head forcing her down onto his dick. He came violently in her mouth. She was choking on his cum and had to swallow it quickly. He held her there sucking his monstrous dick for a bit longer. He stopped her, dragged her to the bed and pushed her down on it. He clambered on top of her and fucked her mercilessly, grunting in pleasure as he satisfied himself. She just lay there and took it. He was every woman's worst nightmare. He just expected her to follow his lead and take his abuse without question, sadistic motherfucker, that he was.

He continued to fuck her like a wild animal. As soon as he calmed down a bit. He got off her, pushed her to one side and lay down. He grunted that she was to get on top of him. She recovered sufficiently to climb on before he had a problem with her pace. Her pussy was so sore. She carefully lowered herself onto his dick. No sooner than he was all in, he started to pummel her mercilessly again. He put his hands on her waits to give himself leverage. He was so strong that he could lift her up and pull her down at will. He kept on fucking her and she was dripping wet. She could hear the sloshing sounds as he rammed her. He slapped her couple of times and kept calling her bitch and whore.

"I am going to fuck you in the ass bitch."

He lifted her completely off his dick. It was dripping with her cunt juice. He entered her ass, grunting loudly as he came close to his orgasm. He pulled her down hard and held her in place as he came. When the orgasm subsided he pulled his dick out of her cock and made her suck it clean. He threw her off him, got out of the bed, got dressed and left without so much as a thank you.

She felt extremely violated. She rested for a bit and then hobbled to the shower. This as a horrible experience for her; She just wanted to go home and crawl into bed and try to forget it all. Unfortunately she had to go to her boss's house first. The clothes that she had left her house in were there and she had to go back home in them or Sanjay would really wonder what she was up to. The chauffeur had been instructed to wait so she met him downstairs.

REALITY CHECK

When she got back to Mr. Flynn's house, he was watching something. She took a closer look and realized that it was her in the video, It was from her first experience with him in his bed and all the other jobs she had done. Somehow, he had taped every encounter she had had. Only her face was visible. The perfect blackmail tape; she could never let her husband find out about this at all. She would be divorced and without friends when they found out she was a highly paid whore.

Her boss was sitting in a chair, watching and stroking himself, waiting for her to get back. He was ready for her and despite her protests that the man that he sent her to was extremely rough and that she was sore, he still wanted his servicing for the evening. He pulled her down into the chair, opened her coat and started to suck her breasts through the lingerie. He was already naked and his cock was beckoning at her. He told her to suck it like a good girl and she got to work. She gave him the best deep throat she could muster after her encounter earlier that evening.

He carried her to the bedroom. He lay down on the bed and made her turn around and mount him so her back was to him. He pulled her back until her pussy was over his mouth. He started to lick her and she was able to continue sucking his dick. He kept licking her wet pussy until she started to grind on his tongue. She was about to have an orgasm. She stopped sucking his dick and surrendered to the feeling. After her pragmatic subsided, she moved down toward his dick. It was so huge, she was sure he would damage her tonight. She had no choice; he had done so much for her.

She started to lower herself onto his dick. She was so sore but she took her time until he was all in. She was sweating profusely. She started to ride, moving up and down on his cock. From time to time she rose up until just the tip was in and then she went back down. He loved when she did this. He was really a great teacher. She was hell-bent on pleasing him. Her aching nipples were hard, her breasts were jumping up and down on her chest. She spun around so she was facing him and started to ride again. He teased her breasts with one hand and reached forward with the other to play with her clit. She could barely stand all the stimulation. She had two orgasms in succession. She did not stop riding him.

She smiled at him a she rode him. She was feeling sensations all over her body. She was free to scream all she wanted and that she did. She kept on going up and down, going harder and harder as she came close to another orgasm, she had another one and passed out again. She was not out for long and he was there waiting. He was still hard and waiting for her to make him cum. He took over thrusting his cock in and out, going deeper and deeper each time. He lifted her up completely and moved her forward in one motion and entered her ass.

It was pretty easy now, as her previous appointments had loosened up her anal cavity quite a bit. He could not get all in and he was trying his hardest to push in. She squirmed quite a bit but he was relentless, he held her still and kept on pushing himself in until he was all in. He kept on ramming her in the ass until he came. He held her there for a bit and then released her. She was spent and her stretched out pussy and ass were extremely sore. She hobbled to the bath and took a quick shower, washing her pussy and ass carefully as they hurt so badly.

She came out, Mr. Flynn was asleep. She got dressed and headed home.

Thankfully, her husband was not an overly curious man. He did not question her not wanting to have sex with him for a few weeks. She told him she had an infection and that he should try to be more hygienic so she didn't get any more. Instead he was apologetic and promised he would do better. She satisfied his needs with blow jobs. He was not driven by sex like her boss was, so he was okay with that. Soon she had recovered completely.

She found however that her pussy was a gaping hole that her husband's dick would get lost in. Her boss's big dick had stretched it out completely. She would have to find a solution for that. In the meantime, she hinted to Sanjay that she would allow him to have anal sex with her. He was excited as it would be his first time. She said it was for her too so he would have to be careful. At least she would be able to keep up the fiasco for a while without letting him find out that she was a high priced call girl for her company's clients and an on call fuck shop for her boss. This was her new life. She had become extremely accustomed to having certain things and she did not know what she would do if she lost them. Plus her boss/boyfriend/pimp had all the ammunition he needed to destroy her life. This was just how it had to be.